i put the fear of méxico in 'em

Matthew Paul Olmos

A SAMUEL FRENCH ACTING EDITION

SAMUELFRENCH.COM
SAMUELFRENCH-LONDON.CO.UK

Copyright © 2014 by Matthew Paul Olmos
Cover Photo: CarrilloPhoto
All Rights Reserved

I PUT THE FEAR OF MÉXICO IN 'EM is fully protected under the copyright laws of the United States of America, the British Commonwealth, including Canada, and all other countries of the Copyright Union. All rights, including professional and amateur stage productions, recitation, lecturing, public reading, motion picture, radio broadcasting, television and the rights of translation into foreign languages are strictly reserved.

ISBN 978-0-573-70199-3

www.SamuelFrench.com
www.SamuelFrench-London.co.uk

For Production Enquiries

United States and Canada
Info@SamuelFrench.com
1-866-598-8449

United Kingdom and Europe
Plays@SamuelFrench-London.co.uk
020-7255-4302

Each title is subject to availability from Samuel French, depending upon country of performance. Please be aware that *I PUT THE FEAR OF MÉXICO IN 'EM* may not be licensed by Samuel French in your territory. Professional and amateur producers should contact the nearest Samuel French office or licensing partner to verify availability.

CAUTION: Professional and amateur producers are hereby warned that *I PUT THE FEAR OF MÉXICO IN 'EM* is subject to a licensing fee. Publication of this play does not imply availability for performance. Both amateurs and professionals considering a production are strongly advised to the appropriate agent before starting rehearsals, advertising, or booking a theatre. A licensing fee must be paid whether the title is presented for charity or gain and whether or not admission is charged. Professional/Stock licensing fees quoted upon application to Samuel French, Inc.

No one shall make any changes in this title for the purpose of production. No part of this book may be reproduced, stored in a retrieval system, or transmitted in any form, by any means, now known or yet to be invented, including mechanical, electronic, photocopying, recording, videotaping, or otherwise, without the prior written permission of the publisher. No one shall upload this title, or part of this title, to any social media websites.

For all enquiries regarding motion picture, television, and other media rights, please contact Samuel French.

MUSIC USE NOTE

Licensees are solely responsible for obtaining formal written permission from copyright owners to use copyrighted music in the performance of this play and are strongly cautioned to do so. If no such permission is obtained by the licensee, then the licensee must use only original music that the licensee owns and controls. Licensees are solely responsible and liable for all music clearances and shall indemnify the copyright owners of the play(s) and their licensing agent, Samuel French, against any costs, expenses, losses and liabilities arising from the use of music by licensees. Please contact the appropriate music licensing authority in your territory for the rights to any incidental music.

IMPORTANT BILLING AND CREDIT REQUIREMENTS

If you have obtained performance rights to this title, please refer to your licensing agreement for important billing and credit requirements.

I PUT THE FEAR OF MÉXICO IN 'EM was first produced by Teatro Vista, at Chicago Dramatists in Chicago, Illinois on November 4, 2012. The performance was directed by Ricardo Gutierrez, with sets by Regina Garcia, costumes by Chirstine Pascual, sound by Christopher Kriz, lighting by Sara Hugley, video by Kyle Hamman, and props by Jamie Karas. The Production Stage Manager was Stephanie Hurovitz. The cast was as follows:

EFREN	Miguel Leonardo Nuñez Natoli
JUANA	Charin Alvarez
JONAH	Bryn W. Packard
ADRAY	Cheryl Graeff
OTHER MEXICANS	Marvin Quijada
VIVIA	Cruz Gonzalez Cade

I PUT THE FEAR OF MÉXICO IN 'EM was developed, in part, with the assistance of the Sundance Institute Theatre Program, with additional support from the Sundance Institute's Time Warner Storytelling Fellowship. It has also been developed, in part, by INTAR Theatre's H.P.R.L. program, Gala Theatre and with special thanks to Nichol Alexander, Mando Alvarado, Teddy Cañez, Audrey Esparza, Maria Helan, Annie Henk, Gabriel Gutierrez, Abel Lopez, José Joaquín Pérez, Debbie Saivetz.

CHARACTERS

EFREN – Mexican, 37
JUANA – Mexican, 30
ADRAY (uh-dray) – güera, 34
JONAH – güero, 34
VIVIA – female
ALL OTHER CHARACTERS – Mexican

SETTING

Tijuana, Mexico

TIME

Now

ACT ONE

(Lights reveal the sort of alley you're not supposed to go down.)

(EFREN corners JONAH and ADRAY against a wall; they wear backpacks and frightened faces.)

(EFREN clears a Tecate, drops the can to the floor, and kicks it at JONAH and ADRAY; they flinch.)

(EFREN laughs his ass off, then looks to JUANA who does not laugh her ass off, but only smiles politely.)

(There are several emptied cans of Tecate around both EFREN and JUANA's feet.)

EFREN. *(to JONAH)* C'mon...I'm not gonna do nuthin'. Hey, c'mere. *(pause)* I wanna know something. *(pause)* C'mon, I just said I won't do nuthin'.

(JONAH reluctantly walks to EFREN.)

So uh...you don't look too comfortable, huh?

JONAH. You could say that.

EFREN. I just did fuckin' say that.

JONAH. What was it you wanted to know?

EFREN. ...so like, if you could like be anywhere but here, where would you be?

JONAH. ...

EFREN. Like right now, if you could disappear someplace, *anyplace*, where would you go to?

JONAH. ...a bar.

EFREN. *(to JUANA)* Hey, Fea, a bar he says.

(EFREN motions for another Tecate, JUANA tosses one to him, he opens, takes a sip, then offers to JONAH, who accepts.)

Ehh, salud. To our wives.

(to ADRAY) Oh shit, wait, you two married?

JONAH. Yea.

EFREN. *(to JONAH)* I wasn't talking to you, was I?

(to ADRAY) You two married?

(ADRAY nods.)

What's a matter, you don't talk? Ain't you gotta tongue? Shit, I'm about to feel lotta sorrow for Jonah here if I hear you don't gotta tongue?

JONAH. She has one.

EFREN. *(to ADRAY)* So why don't she talk then, I ask you a question, why don't you talk.

JONAH. She talks.

EFREN. I ain't ask you, did I.

JONAH. Adray, will you...

EFREN. *(to ADRAY)* Hey, yoo-hoo, Little Thing...I hear you got a good tongue in that mouth. ...why don't you lemme see that purty tongue, huh? Awh, what's a matter, Little Thing, you a shy one? Hmm?

(to JUANA) Hey, Fea, why don'you show Little Thing here about what kinda tongue *we* got.

(JUANA shows the entire of her tongue.)

(to ADRAY) Now you see that, tha's the kinda tongue a man can come home to. Wake up with. Tha's the kinda tongue make a man stay put for life. *(pause)* So why don't you show me what your husband come home to...

JONAH. Mister uh, Efren, can I get another?

(A moment of EFREN sizing up JONAH.)

EFREN. Fea, the man ordered up, huh.

(JUANA *pulls a fresh Tecate.*)

JONAH. *(to* JUANA*)* It's for her.

(JUANA *tosses the beer to* ADRAY, *she catches, drinks.*)

EFREN. *(to* ADRAY*)* Tha's some kinda gentle man you got there, Little Thing. *(pause)* Always comin' home good an' early. *(pause)* Never lay a hand, raise a fist. *(pause)* Never got lipstick on his neck, never got other-women-scent on his fingers. *(pause)*

Always make sure you cum. Every time.

*(*EFREN *waits for response.)*

Yea, with a man like that you must get real, real thankful, yea? *(pause)*

How thankful?

*(*ADRAY *pulls in Tecate, then sticks her tongue out at* EFREN.*)*

Oh. Little Thing you ain't so little. Will you lookit that, Fea. What's a little güera like you doin' with a lengüita like that, huh?

(to JONAH*)* Shit, no wonder you treat her so good. Hey, how is it, her lengüita? Is it fast? Does it circle around down there? Does it do tricks?

JONAH. You said imagine we were at a bar.

EFREN. You know what, you're right. Know what happened? I got whatsitcalled…side tracked, yea? *(pause)* Okay, okay, so picture just us two, we're in a bar sitting. We got our legs open, we got our Tecates in hand. An' know what? Just for picture's sake, there's a fútbol game, huh? *(pause)* What? You wan' something else, beisbol?

JONAH. Soccer's fine.

EFREN. Okay, so we can watch "soccer" on the T.V. *(pause)* An' do you know what I like the best about two men talking good with each other at a bar?

JONAH. That we don't have to—

EFREN. That we're honest. *(pause)* Women don't give a shit, they'll tell to each other whatever the fuck, but men, we say the truth to each other, huh?

JONAH. Yea.

EFREN. So do you know what I would like to ask, at this bar, with our Tecates, watchin' our fútbol, huh? *(pause)* What I would like to ask is…How Is Your Wife's Tongue?

(EFREN puts his hand on JONAH's shoulder.)

JONAH. It's…fine.

EFREN. Is it fast?

JONAH. It can be.

EFREN. Does it circle around down there?

JONAH. If she's in the mood, yes.

EFREN. Yes?

JONAH. It does.

EFREN. Does what?

JONAH. Circle around down there.

EFREN. An' does it do tricks?

JONAH. None that I know of.

EFREN. Does It Do Tricks.

JONAH. …she used to, she…used to use the bottom of it, of her tongue. The underneath. Was softer.

EFREN. Thank you, Mister Jonah. For bein' honest with me.

(EFREN and JONAH share a moment. EFREN's phone rings; they both notice. Lights focus on JUANA, who stands up allowing us to see clearly that she has had an assault rifle hanging from her shoulder the entire time. She walks to ADRAY and speaks to her closely.)

JUANA. *(to ADRAY)* That shit all true, güera? 'Bout usin' the bottom part uh your lengüita? That shit really work? *(pause)* Wow. You know what I think, though? If you use the bottom, es like you can't really taste what you're putting your tongue to? 'Cuz even if mi Efren don't always taste so good, I like to know es him I'm making happy. So maybe is it you use the bottom 'cuz es softer, or 'cuz you don't like to taste? *(pause)* You're not gonna respond to me, huh? *(pause)* Tha's okay, I know es hard to have a real, honest conversation between adults if one of you…

(JUANA *holds up the machine gun awkwardly.*)

Efren says it to me that I haffta hold the gun 'cuz why, Feo?

EFREN. Equal rights.

JUANA. He's so stupid. Between you an' me, güera, I think it just turn him on. A woman, a gun, sometimes I think I never understand the men. *(pause)* For truth tho', güera, lookit me, I don't understand the gun either. I leave it on "safety" an' there's nothing he could say to me that I'd set it to unsafety. *(pause)* Know what tho'? I like holdin' it. Heavy. I feel like you hear me, you know? But maybe that's not such a good thing, huh, feeling finally like you listen, 'cuz me I'm holding in my hands something that was not meant for talking.

Es like earlier today when we tried to speak to you. What? You don't remember? *(pause)* Over by where all that shit with the red buses. I know I seen your eyes pass over us when come up close to you. I guess we were just one small part of your foto background. But when we try to speak, when we try to ask if you need help, you yank your husband away from us like he the one that be needing the help. An' lookit you now, now you do need help, don't you? Both of you, and yea, güera, I bet if you take a foto now, we won't be background no more. But not because we equal. Es just because you're scared. That we might shoot you.

(JONAH *enters* JUANA *and* ADRAY*'s light.*)

For truth tho', güera, I don't know how people do it. Los Narcos. Los Soldados. Los Policias. Es only for our son, Javier, he's thirteen, for mi Javi that I holding this gun.

JONAH. We have a daughter. Angela. She's close to your Javier's age. She's home. Alone. We promised to call three times daily. We did this morning, but…this morning feels like a lot of days ago.

(Lights shift to several hours before. **ADRAY** *and* **JONAH** *are both on their mobiles in a San Ysidro Motel 6. A moment. They both hang up.)*

ADRAY. Angela says she's in love.

JONAH. Mexicoach says there's won't be any buses at *all* today.

ADRAY. She wanted to wait till we were away. That I'm judgmental.

JONAH. Apparently there's some sort of glitch. Like in all the buses. The entire fleet; some sort of mechanical failure?

ADRAY. Some boy who sits in the back of the class. Shy.

JONAH. She called you that? Judgmental?

ADRAY. So, what, there's no tour buses anywhere? Thank God.

JONAH. Service on indefinite hiatus.

ADRAY. She said 'cuz I always roll my eyes at those movies you two like.

JONAH. All that shit you talked about the red buses an' here ya go, I hope yer happy.

ADRAY. Jonah, I just don't want our daughter growing up thinking that's what love is gonna—

JONAH. What, an' we're not romantic?

ADRAY. Are we?

JONAH. I proposed to you at the top of—

ADRAY. That's different.

JONAH. You cried.

ADRAY. I had bites on my ankles. I was hungover from that forty percent bullshit you got suckered into. Your breath was stale, sorry. Movies don't ever show any of that, but that's what love is like.

JONAH. You were also on your period.

(They share a laugh.)

ADRAY. See, it's a sign, Jones, we argue all over the little red buses an' now lookit us.

JONAH. Yea, you got your way. Again.

ADRAY. Oh, shut up. C'mere.

(She pulls him in for a kiss.)

So that website said we could just take one of the sidestreets off that Revolution street, down a little hill and there'll be like multiple cars.

JONAH. It said there'd be station wagons, Adray.

ADRAY. Yea, station wagons driven by actual citizens, like real people...

JONAH. You're doing the talking.

ADRAY. "Yo queiro ir a Ensenada."

JONAH. You have to say it in 'we' form.

ADRAY. I'm sure they'll get it.

JONAH. Adray, the website didn't say anything about driving us back.

ADRAY. Jones, we were stupid in Marseille, this time I have the public transport schedule printed out, we have the street map—

JONAH. This isn't fucking France, you know. How fucking accurate do you think a public transportation print out is?

ADRAY. Well, it's only a hundred and ten kilometers from Tijuana, even if it's all-the-way backwards, I'm sure we can—

JONAH. Miles. It's seventy miles, okay. You're not European.

ADRAY. Jones, c'mon, it'll be just you an' me. That dirt road we saw on that one website. We'll push past all the beer cans and left diapers— What? What's the matter?

JONAH. It's just with Mexicoach there was a credit card record of where we were going. What bus times? If anything happened Angela could at least—

ADRAY. C'mon, Jones, a little off-the-map between consenting adults...

JONAH. If you think I'm doing *anything* in public, in fucking Mexico...

ADRAY. Just knowing that like...even satellites couldn't trace us. God, it's so...real.

JONAH. Yea, satellites don't cover Mexico, I forgot. Alright, so fine, I'll go along with the station wagons, but we are *getting off* at that little lobster town whatever.

ADRAY. ...fine, *when* we resurface, we'll visit yer little Puerto Nuevo tourist bullshit people acting like they don't have a goddamned ocean at home.

JONAH. I like the idea of fried lobster. Langosta.

ADRAY. You like romantic comedies.

JONAH. So what else'd she say, she didn't wanna talk to me?

ADRAY. Know what does scare me though, Jones? *(pause)* How much her heart will be broken. How many hearts she'll break. It's like until today, she was safe. That boy in the back of the class was safe. But now...I almost wish it she would wait. Just get a couple more years of being untouched.

JONAH. Touched, she said touched?

ADRAY. No, not *touched*.

JONAH. Oh. Well...I think it's cute then. Her, some boy. I'm glad he's shy.

ADRAY. Awh, maybe he's just like—

JONAH. Well would you rather him be, what, forward?

ADRAY. No, I wish...I just didn't think we'd have to deal with this so—

JONAH. Her heart is open, Adray, least we know it works.

ADRAY. What was that, a line from movie? My God.

JONAH. Shut up.

ADRAY. Look, after lunch, why don't you call her? See if she tells it to you any different. "Her heart is open..."

JONAH. Just don't forget the phone card.

ADRAY. Got.

JONAH. Hey, really, why don't we just take one of our phones, it's stupid not to.

ADRAY. Oh God, my wife's a fucking tourist too. Way to disconnect, Jonah.

JONAH. You know Mexicans do have cell phones, Adray.

ADRAY. And I'm not judging, y'know. That she thinks she's in love.

(beat)

JONAH. Well, I just hope this Nepalese statue is as off the map as Google said it was.

ADRAY. Oh, shut up, how else are you supposed to—

JONAH. Yea, yea, just don't forget your underground website print outs, Miss Native of México.

ADRAY. Don't worry, they're in my bag right next to your balls, Princessa.

*(Lights up on a bar, cheap strobe effects and twitching neon. **JONAH** sits, he looks about a bit lost. A salted margarita on ice gets placed in front of him. He looks at it surprised, sniffs. As he confusedly takes a sip, a souvenir, straw cowboy hat with red bandana reading: "Viva Tijuana!" is placed on his head, he looks to see who placed it, but no one is there. **JONAH** clears his margarita and watches in disbelief as he is refilled. **JUANA** takes a seat next to him. He looks at her strangely.)*

(Lights shift back to alley.)

EFREN. You're never going to believe this, Little Thing.

ADRAY. Where's Jonah, is he okay?

EFREN. He's in a bar, just like he wished for. So, know what you ain't gonna believe?

ADRAY. A bar where?

EFREN. Me, I just got off the phone. Mi Javier, he calls me like multiple times a day, little shit misses me I guess. But do you know what he call me about today?

ADRAY. What bar?

EFREN. There's lots of bars in Tijuana, güera, an' I bet you couldn't tell the difference between one of'em. *(pause)* So…he say that some girl, some little güerita who sits in front uh the class, is top-of-the-heap-in-love with him. Can you believe that?

ADRAY. …I'd like to go the bar where my husband's at.

EFREN. No, you don't. I know you didn't come down here for that.

ADRAY. Well, I'm sure he'd rather be here with his wife—

EFREN. When Mister Jonah wants to be here with you, güera, he will be.

*(Lights brighten over **JONAH**, as he's served two margaritas. He drinks ravenously. **JUANA** watches him.)*

(Lights dim over the bar.)

EFREN. So Javier, he loves to sit in the back of the class. Well, I don't know that he loves it, more like…he prefers to sit in the back of the class. Hey, you listening?

ADRAY. …yea.

EFREN. So there he is just sittin', and this little güera comes on up to him, an— oh shit, wait, you know what a güera is?

ADRAY. I get the implication.

EFREN. So what is it then?

ADRAY. A…a woman who's white…but clearly not welcome.

EFREN. Oh, no, es not like that. Es just, yea somebody like you, but… güera don't mean you're not welcome.

ADRAY. Thank you.

EFREN. Where was I?

ADRAY. The back of the class.

EFREN. So some güerita comes up to mi Javi, right in the middle of some movie they're showing. Plate teh'tonics or…how's it called—

ADRAY. Plate tectonics.

EFREN. You know?

ADRAY. Yes, I know what it is, go on.

EFREN. So what is it then?

ADRAY. It's...it's the movement of the plates, like continents...away from each other. Like from Pangaea, I suppose.

EFREN. Pan-wha?

ADRAY. Pangaea. It's when, it's the belief that all the continents or—

EFREN. All six.

ADRAY. Anyways, Pangaea is one of the theories that all the plates, or continents, were...all together at one point.

EFREN. Well Javi didn't say nuthin'about that.

ADRAY. Maybe wasn't paying attention—

JAVIER. Yea, or maybe he jus'don't give a fuck about continents.

ADRAY. Okay.

EFREN. So anyways, right when the classroom is all dark... this little güera comes up and sits in the empty seat next to him. Smiling that smile. You know?

ADRAY. I think so.

EFREN. Hey, how come girls smile like that, huh?

ADRAY. ...I guess they want to seem welcoming.

EFREN. Hey, "welcoming," we were just talking about, huh?

ADRAY. We were.

EFREN. So...she leans over right close into his ear and says... "I think I'm in love with you, Javier." *(laughs)* Can you believe in that?

ADRAY. If you say so.

(EFREN takes ADRAY softly by the hand, she reacts, but he motions her to relax.)

EFREN. An' then, know what? Mi Javier took her hand out into the hallway where nobody is and nobody's supposed to be.

(Lights turn young, EFREN leads ADRAY to a corner spot. They speak as teenagers.)

"Don't worry, no one will come. No one will see."

ADRAY. "But we shouldn't—"

EFREN. "Shh....I wanted to bring you here, Angela, because I didn't want anyone to hear what I want to tell you."

ADRAY. "...tell me...?"

EFREN. "Do you know why I sit in the back of the class all the time?"

(ADRAY *shakes her head.*)

"It's 'cuz I'm afraid."

ADRAY. "Of what?"

EFREN. "Like if I sit too up close that..."

ADRAY. "What?"

EFREN. "That I won't be able to look at you. That you'll see me looking. That you'll know."

ADRAY. "Know what?"

EFREN. "...how I feel."

ADRAY. "...how do you feel?"

EFREN. "I feel like when I wake up, I only do it 'cuz I wanna see what you'll be wearing. I feel like when I get ready for school, I'm really gettin' ready for you."

ADRAY. "...you never told me..."

EFREN. "Can...can I kiss you?"

(ADRAY *nods.* EFREN *kisses her.*)

"Know what I think about?"

(ADRAY *shakes her head.*)

EFREN. "Promise you won't make fun, promise it will be our secret, just yours and mine."

ADRAY. "I promise."

EFREN. "I think about what it would be like to touch you... like underneath."

ADRAY. "Me?"

EFREN. "So...soft. So clean."

ADRAY. "...well, maybe...maybe you could put your hand..."

EFREN. "You aren't teasin', are you?"

ADRAY. "…I wouldn't tease, not with you. Here, you can…"

(**EFREN** *gently puts his hand up* **ADRAY**'s *shirt. She allows. They both enjoy for a few innocent moments.*)

EFREN. "Do you have brothers?"

(**ADRAY** *shakes her head.*)

"Have you ever seen it?"

ADRAY. "What?"

EFREN. "It."

ADRAY. "No, omigod, of course not."

EFREN. "Do you want to?"

ADRAY. "No, what if somebody comes?"

EFREN. "See, it's got all hard now. Because of you."

ADRAY. "Omigod."

EFREN. "I want you to."

ADRAY. "No, really we should—"

(**EFREN** *offers her a peek down into his pants. She glimpses.*)

"…it looks…crowded. Are you sure there's enough room down there for it?"

EFREN. "You can touch it if you want to."

(**ADRAY** *takes a few moments, then dips her hand in.* **EFREN** *closes his eyes, she watches him, then touches more. She kisses him.*)

"So…you've seen mine…I've never seen what yours looks like. I don't have any sisters."

ADRAY. "Well…I can't show you *here.*"

EFREN. "What if I just like peek in. Like you did.

ADRAY. "I don't think you'll be able to see like that."

(**EFREN** *kneels.*)

"No, c'mon."

EFREN. "Please, just for real quick."

> (ADRAY *gives* EFREN *a peek, then reaching out to touch, she allows. He explores. She closes her eyes.* EFREN *stands up and returns her hand between his legs with his between hers. They both close their eyes. A few beautiful moments of connection. Then interruption,* EFREN *opens his eyes.)*

"Shit. Somebody's coming."

> *(He pulls his pants up and walks away.)*

"C'mon."

ADRAY. "But…"

> *(She looks at her hand. Smells. Then wipes it on her clothes embarrassed, then looks around nervously.)*
> *(Lights shift,* EFREN *resumes his usual voice.)*

EFREN. With a morning like that, I can't even guess what the rest of their day was like, huh.

ADRAY. Can I please use your phone.

EFREN. …

ADRAY. I'd like to call my daughter.

EFREN. Ta say what?

ADRAY. To see how she is.

EFREN. I just tol'you how she is.

ADRAY. Please.

EFREN. What, you don't believe me?

ADRAY. Can I make my call or can't I?

EFREN. You think I was just makin'that story up for your amusements?

ADRAY. I have a calling card.

EFREN. Congratulations.

ADRAY. It won't cost you any money.

EFREN. What will it cost then?

ADRAY. I just want talk to my daughter.

EFREN. What, I ain't reliable?

ADRAY. Thank you anyway.

EFREN. What will it cost me, güera?

ADRAY. I'm not calling, so nothing I guess.

EFREN. If I let you make that call, that'd be saying that the story I told you, about mi Javier and your Angela, was untrue.

ADRAY. What do you want? If you want money, it's yours.

(**ADRAY** *throws her wallet at* **EFREN**.)

If you want to embarrass us, you have.

EFREN. What I want, Little Thing, is for you to believe in a world of continents where a little girl like your Angela and a boy like mi Javier could and would sneak themselves into the hallway. How you say, "lose their innocence" together, yea? That that could happen.

ADRAY. Why don't you leave my daughter out of whatever it is you're doing? Please.

EFREN. That boy, in the back of the class, do you know his name?

ADRAY. What?

EFREN. Your daughter. She's in love with some boy. Back of the class. Do you know his fucking name?

ADRAY. ...no, I do not.

EFREN. Could it be Javier?

ADRAY. ...

EFREN. So how do you know it wasn't him? How do you know my boy and your girl didn't get their paws an' mittens mixed up this morning?

ADRAY. Well, for one they live in different countries.

EFREN. So? You an' me are different countries, but here we are. Talking intimately about intimate things. Hell, we might as well be rubbing our paws an' mittens too.

ADRAY. It'd be a little hard for your Javier and my Angela to be in the same school, wouldn't it?

EFREN. Did I tell you what school mi Javier attends?

ADRAY. ...does it matter?

(**EFREN** *hands her the phone.*)

EFREN. Use your fucking calling card.

(**ADRAY** *takes a moment, then pulls a card and begins the process.*)

ADRAY. *(into phone)* Hey, kiddo, what're you— *(pause)* Oh, I'm glad I caught you then. *(pause)* We're at...we're outside shopping. Are you...okay, everything's usual as usual? *(pause)* Yea, I'll see what we can find, okay. *(pause)* I know, I know. Listen, Angela, that uh...boy you told me about this morning. Did you see him, I mean was he at school— *(pause)* I'm just curious is all. *(pause)* Did...did he talk to you, I mean did you get to talk to him today? *(pause)* What's a matter, you sound nervous. *(pause)* No, your voice just...must be the connection. *(pause)* An' you think he likes you, yea? *(pause)* So...what's his name anyways? *(pause)* Oh. And...um...what's his first name then...?

(long godawful pause)

...okay look, uh, I lost your dad, I gotta run. I'll call you later, okay? I will. I know. Bye, baby.

(**ADRAY** *lowers phone, closing it.*)

EFREN. What's a matter, Little Thing, you're lookin'at me like you know me.

ADRAY. Who are you?

EFREN. Me, I'm just some mejicano nobody.

ADRAY. How do you know my daughter?

EFREN. Me, I never met her myself.

ADRAY. Where did you get that story from?

EFREN. Mi Javier tol' me.

ADRAY. What school does your son go to?

EFREN. Dos Pueblos.

ADRAY. ...how do you know that name?

EFREN. Don't most parents know the school their kid goes?

ADRAY. How do you know who my... *(pause)* ...how do you know that name?

EFREN. We're not so far apart, Little Thing. I know there's supposed ta be an iron'steel wall between us. But see, your Angela—

ADRAY. Don't say her name—

EFREN. Your Angela and mi Javi. They're not tall enough to know about any iron'steel wall between them. They don't have anything between them. Not yet. They get up, they go to school. They're just little kids every day, but they're also not just little kids every day. *(pause)* Me, I don't find it such a strange thing that they got a whatcha'muh'callit…a shared experience. I'm glad Javier's Dos Pueblos and your Angela's Dos Pueblos are like one fucking pueblo.

ADRAY. We haven't done anything to you.

EFREN. An' me, what have I done to you?

ADRAY. You grabbed us—

EFREN. NO, no we didn't grab no one—

ADRAY. You forced us into this alley—

EFREN. We asked.

ADRAY. Your wife pointed a machine gun at us.

EFREN. Yes. Yes, okay, my wife did point a machine gun—

ADRAY. We didn't mean anything by…

EFREN. Why did you get off the main street?

ADRAY. Excuse me?

EFREN. You heard me.

ADRAY. We wanted to…that statue…on the way to Ensenada. We were taking one of those station wagons at the bottom of the hill—

EFREN. Why didn't you just wait for the red buses like everybody else?

ADRAY. We just didn't.

EFREN. Why not?

ADRAY. There wasn't any red buses, we talked to Mexicoach, there was some glitch, some mechanical failure—

EFREN. So, if there was no "glitch" or "mechanical failures" you would not be here with me?

ADRAY. …if it were up to me, I don't know where I'd be.

EFREN. Let's just pretend for talking sake then, güera, that things *are* up to you.

ADRAY. …I was glad the buses broke down. I don't like going places that way.

EFREN. What way?

ADRAY. That…packaged way.

EFREN. Oh…so you *wanted* to be walking down that street with no one around an' be crawling into the back of some shitty little station wagon all crowded.

ADRAY. Yes. I did.

EFREN. Well then you should thank me, Little Thing. This is like un'packaged as shit. Look at how close everything is. You and me here. My wife and your husband there. My son and your daughter, look how close we all have come. *(pause)* This is what you wanted, no? This is the kind of story you wish to go back with, eh? Machine guns an' real locals telling you real local things. Drunken Mejicanos. An alleyway. There's even a little sexuality, huh? Little bit. Teenage.

ADRAY. Look, you can think what you wish about me. That's fine. But don't talk about my daughter. I'm asking you.

(EFREN looks at her. A moment.)

And…okay, look if you need me to go to an ATM or—

EFREN. Oh, c'mon now Little Thing, let the assholes who hang out on La Revolución play with the money. Let them be cliché.

ADRAY. Well, what is it you—

EFREN. Me? I just want what you do, güera. What everybody want. To get close. To be less alone.

(ADRAY covers her body and turns away from EFREN.)

Oh Little Thing, you don't have to worry about that. I don't even like güeras. All güeras ever do is…just lay there. *(pause)* What, you don't? You don't just lay yourself down and let whatever just—

ADRAY. I *never* just lay there.

(Lights shift to **JONAH** *and* **JUANA**, *several empty margarita and shot glasses in front of them.)*

JUANA. So, this is what you would do tho', ehh? If your vacación were up to you, this is where you would be, no?

JONAH. Maybe.

JUANA. What you mean "maybe?" I jus'asked you a question what you want. How can you say "maybe?" *(pause)* What, you don't wanna talk to me?

JONAH. I think I'd need a little more than Cuervo shots and margaritas to put me in the mood for anything besides wanting to go the fuck home.

JUANA. Tha's funny. Most people, they come here, they drink Cuervo shots an' margaritas and they get in the mood to never wanna go home.

JONAH. Well most people don't get held up by fucking gunpoint an hour after they cross the border.

JUANA. No, but some do though, huh? *(pause)* Mister Jonah, you say if you could be anywhere in the world, you would be in a bar. An' here you are. Sitting with tequila sliding down the bar to you, with margaritas always filled up. This is what people pay good money for, well, maybe not *good* money, but they pay a little money, huh, like bargain.

JONAH. Yea, this has all been just fucking fantastic. You two should offer your personal fucking machine gun service to more tourists, really.

JUANA. So tell me, Mister Jonah, why did you not bring your Angela?

JONAH. What?

JUANA. Was my English confusing?

JONAH. Why did you ask that?

JUANA. Why did you not answer?

JONAH. Look, what is this?

JUANA. What is what?

JONAH. This. You hold me an' my wife up, you scare the shit out of us, and now what, you wanna drink with me? You wanna talk with me?

JUANA. I was just curious. Angela. So close to mi Javi's age. At home alone. An' that you call to her three times a day, like you are scared for her to be safe, but…

JONAH. But what?

JUANA. If you are so scared that she will not be okay, why did you leave her then? Why do you not bring her to things?

JONAH. We don't not bring her.

JUANA. You didn't come here to drink in the bars, you didn't come here to dance all night. And, I don' know if this is for truth or not, but it don't look like you two came here to be…

JONAH. Be what?

JUANA. A man an' woman.

JONAH. Okay, you know what? Why don't you drop talking about my family, alright? You don't hear me talking about yours.

JUANA. You don't know mine.

JONAH. An' that's fine with me.

JUANA. You are not curious?

JONAH. No, I am not curious.

JUANA. How come?

(**JONAH** *drinks, ignores.*)

Ay, Jonah, lo siento. I didn't mean to say about how you leave your daughter places. I just feel bad for her, tha's how come.

JONAH. *My daughter* has fucking school, okay?

JUANA. Ahh, so tha's how come? Si, yo entiendo. Her education was "the most important thing."

(**JONAH** *finishes his drink, ignores.*)

Angelita…I would like to meet her someday.

JONAH. Okay, maybe this is a me thing, but I don't like hearing strangers talk about my daughter so...familiar.

JUANA. Me, I don't know your Angelita. I am not familiar.

JONAH. Exactly.

JUANA. But are you?

JONAH. Look, the only reason I even mentioned we *had* a daughter was just in case you two had some sort of conscience.

JUANA. Es okay, you know. I know it is hard to be close to your children.

JONAH. Just because we didn't bring our daughter to fucking Mexico doesn't mean— ...this is ridiculous.

JUANA. What is?

JONAH. That we're even—

JUANA. Even what?

JONAH. That I'm sitting in fucking Tijuana talking about my daughter with you.

JUANA. We're just two parents talking about our children, güero. So...

JONAH. So what?

JUANA. You were scared she would slow you down? That she would see things not good for kids?

JONAH. ...yes, to both, I guess.

JUANA. ...if ugly is how you an' your wife see things here in México, why do you come?
(pause) Or maybe it is just your wife. Whatever güerita want, güerita get, huh?

JONAH. Look, I agreed to come because I wanted to, okay. I *wanted* to come here. An', what, just because you meet my wife for—

JUANA. What.

JONAH. It's not whatever she wants.

JUANA. No?

JONAH. An'...

JUANA. What, say it, Jonah.

JONAH. Despite what you may think, Adray is a wonderful mother.

JUANA. An' you? *(pause)* Are you a *wonderful* father?

(**JONAH** *drinks*)

Well, my hope is that you both are, equally, the most wonderful parents that could be. *(pause)* What? What is it?

(beat)

JONAH. …when Angie was a uh…when we finally put her crib in the other room…you know she'd cry. She'd be so loud, that if we were sleeping of course we'd wake up. We'd—

JUANA. I get it.

JONAH. Right, so do you know what I would do?

JUANA. You tell me.

JONAH. I would just leave her there. With my eyes shut. With my breathing as if I was sleeping. I would stay like that until Adray got up and checked on her herself. I didn't want to deal with it.

JUANA. So, you're lazy.

JONAH. No, see every time Angela'd cry, always I would have these nightmares in my head that I'd walk into her room, peer over the rail and…the loose end of a blanket stifling her breathing. A toy sticking out of her mouth. Blood *anywhere* in that crib. And so instead of getting out of bed and picking Angela up, I would leave her for Adray to deal with. It made more sense for Adray to curse me under her tired breath and think me the laziest son of a bitch that ever laid horizontal than to wake up to nightmares like those ones.

(beat)

JUANA. Do you know what parenting is?

JONAH. Making sure your children have better than you did.

JUANA. No, that's a result of parenting.

JONAH. *You're* gonna tell me what parenting—
JUANA. An' what the fuck does that mean?
JONAH. …
JUANA. Well…
JONAH. You're holding a machine gun.
JUANA. So. Did I shoot you?
JONAH. No.
JUANA. You listen to me, huh. Every night I say the prayers and lose at least one hour sleep for my boy. An' d'you know how come?

(JONAH *shakes his head.*)

Because I worry. Because that's what parenting is. It's worry. Worrying about somebody else's life in front of yer own. *(pause)* You can fuck up. You can make the mistakes. But if you don't let your worry guide you in everything that you do…then you're separate from your children and what good are you?
JONAH. I worry about Angela.
JUANA. But you also run from her.
JONAH. My worrying'll only worry her.
JUANA. And one day she'll run from things the same that you do.
JONAH. Or maybe she won't. Maybe she'll look at me and do better than I did.
JUANA. You need to face your daughter Angela, no matter how ugly you imagine things to be. Otherwise she'll grow up thinking you only like the pretty parts of her, when she has no troubles. Otherwise you'll be a tourist in your own daughter's life.
JONAH. *(to bar)* Can I get another fucking margarita, blended with no fucking salt, please.
JUANA. Why not have a shot on top.
JONAH. And another Cuervo Gold, this time chilled, por favor. Can I get that muy rapido, please!

JUANA. Your drink. Drinks. Are there.

    (JONAH *drinks.*)

Mi Javier fell in love today. With some girl front of the class.

    (JONAH *spits up, stares at* JUANA. *A moment. Lights shift to behind them, a spotlight and smoke rise on a pole. A strip club pole to be exact. A young girl,* VIVIA, *who is about nineteen, but could easily play fourteen in a movie, walks up to the pole and tries to maneuver it. Fails. She tries again. Fails. She tries one last time before failing and hurrying off the stage. Lights shift back to the bar.*)

JONAH. Who the fuck are you?

JUANA. Just some ridiculous mejicana, I guess.

JONAH. I'm going.

JUANA. Where, back to the alley? Un momento por favor, let me just grab the machine gun then.

JONAH. What Do You Want.

JUANA. For you to be okay with mi Javier.

JONAH. Fine, I'm okay with Javier.

JUANA. With your Angela.

JONAH. I told you not to use her fucking name.

JUANA. Why don't you order another.

    (*He does.*)

JONAH. Where the fuck am I?

JUANA. This is a bar in Tijuana, where the fuck are you.

    (*Enter* VIVIA. *She walks to him.*)

VIVIA. Hello. I Vivia.

JONAH. Uh, Jonah. …hi.

VIVIA. Do you…want to…?

    (VIVIA *looks towards the back of the room.*)

JONAH. Um…thank you, I'm okay.

VIVIA. Oh. *(pause)* They make us ask. Es okay if you don't want.

JONAH. ...gracias...

VIVIA. Would you like to know something?

JONAH. I'm actually not here to...

VIVIA. I don't know how the pole work? For the job, they just say show up. They think you will already know.

JONAH. I...I'm sorry.

VIVIA. They should let you come with them the night before an' let you sit up close to it. So that you can see how they do.

JONAH. Yea, I guess so.

VIVIA. Can I have a drink with you?

JONAH. ...look—

VIVIA. *(whispering)* We are supposed to say that too.

JONAH. Fine.

(A drinks slides in front of **VIVIA.***)*

VIVIA. Thank you, Mister... *(pause)* So, eh...I shy.

JONAH. ...me too.

VIVIA. ...I know because I don't have many clothes on that I don't look like I shy, but...

JONAH. *(to* JUANA*)* Can we???

JUANA. This ain't got nothin' to do with me, güero.

VIVIA. Es okay if you don't like me.

JONAH. You're fine.

VIVIA. But no to the back?

JONAH. No to the back.

VIVIA. I am supposed to keep asking. About you and me going to the back. See, es just right there, not so far. Psst, Mister Johah, we could just pretend to go to the back and—

JONAH. Look I'm not gonna go to the back in fucking Mexico!

*(***VIVIA** *puts down her drink and begins to leave.)*

Shit, hey...

VIVIA. No, yo entiendo. I don't know how to work the pole, I don't know how to wear these things I wear, ja I understand you don't want to go to the back with me. But do you know something, Mister Jonah?

JONAH. I didn't mean to—

VIVIA. I'm not the one drinking Tequilas at a bar with a pole in it.

JONAH. ...I shouldnt've raised my voice.

VIVIA. You sit here an' you look just like all the other men that sit here. But when I try to talk, when I try to do my job, you answer to me like I'm the one who don't belong.

JONAH. ...

VIVIA. But if you don't want to belong here, why did you come?

(beat)

JONAH. Please, Vivia, finish your drink.

VIVIA. ...

JONAH. Salud.

(They clink awkwardly. A moment.)

VIVIA. Do you see how these clothes are like...too tight, see I can barely fit myself inside them...see, how I spill out...

*(**VIVIA** shows him the elastic of her outfit. She waits. And waits. Finally, he embarrassedly places several dollars underneath it. She sits back down. **JONAH** looks at the two women sitting on either side of him and wonders how the fuck he got there.)*

*(Lights switch to **EFREN** and **ADRAY** in the alley.)*

ADRAY. Not even when I was a teenager and didn't know what the fuck I was doing. I *never* just laid there. Not even when I was scared as shit.

EFREN. Hey, tha's yer husband's problems, not mine.

ADRAY. ...can I get one of those Tecates?

(EFREN *tosses one to her. She catches.*)

EFREN. Man up.

(ADRAY *clears it.*)

ADRAY. Más?

EFREN. Fuck that.

(EFREN *pulls a cheap, mini-souvenir bottle of Gusano Rojo Mezcal*)

ADRAY. What's that?

EFREN. Authentic shit.

ADRAY. Is that with the worm?

EFREN. Do I haffta dangle it in front of you, or are you gonna come an' bite already?

(EFREN *tosses to* ADRAY. *She opens and sniffs.*)

Hey, it ain't for smellin', it's for pourin'over that tongue.

(ADRAY *clears it.*)

ADRAY. Otro más.

(EFREN *tosses another. She opens.*)

Ain't you havin' any?

(EFREN *laughs.*)

EFREN. No gracias.

(EFREN *coughs up, he pounds his chest, trying to swallow.*)

ADRAY. You okay? What is—

(EFREN *takes control, cracks a Tecate, and drowns. When he is done, he notices* ADRAY *looking at him. A moment.*)

What was that?

EFREN. You ever get this...

(EFREN *touches his chest.* ADRAY *looks confused.*)

Es nada.

(**EFREN** *clears his drink,* **ADRAY** *gets him another, he takes it. A moment.*)

ADRAY. So here we are. We got our Tecates in hand. We got our wives someplace else.

EFREN. Salud, to our wifes someplace else…

ADRAY. …Mister Efren…can I ask you honestly?

EFREN. I don' know, can you?

ADRAY. See, I can be here with you, I can drink with you. I can do my best not to be just some stupid güera. But I need to ask you.

EFREN. So ask.

ADRAY. I need to ask if you're going to… Whatever the answer may be. I don't even care what it is. Just…*are you going to hurt us?* *(pause)* You can just say it. Say it to me like I'm not even listening.

EFREN. You are a strange fuckin'white lady.

ADRAY. This is honesty, right, isn't that what you're looking for?

EFREN. Si, pero…is that what you're doing, huh? Yer bein' honest with me, güera?

ADRAY. I'm trying.

EFREN. Drinkin'with me, talking with me how you don't just lay there. This is how you are for reals?

ADRAY. Well what would you like to see? Would you like me to speak up to you, answer whatever macho bullshit question you throw out there like my husband? Hmm? Would you like me frightened in the corner? Is that what *you* think *we* all do?

EFREN. You know what's like universal?

ADRAY. What?

EFREN. Women. They never want to be like other women.

ADRAY. Okay…

EFREN. Always they want to be like the exception to the expectation. Louder than people think they are, an' more thoughtful then people assume. Here you are in Tijuana, away from your husband and you're doing everything you can think to prove to me that you don't come from a long line, is that how you say, of women who just lay there. But really, what do you care?

ADRAY. I don't. I know you lookit me an' see something you can just roll over. But that's not me.

EFREN. ...*I don't know.*

ADRAY. What?

EFREN. I was answering to you your question: I don't know.

(**ADRAY** *reacts. Enter* **MARIACHI GUITAR PLAYER**. *He begins to play.* **EFREN** *suggests to* **ADRAY** *to engage with the music. She questions; he insists.* **ADRAY** *attempts to move to the music. She is out of tune, so* **EFREN** *leads and they move together. The song softens to a ballad;* **MARIACHI** *sings softly to* **ADRAY** *and* **EFREN** *places her arms around him. A moment.* **EFREN** *pulls* **ADRAY** *closer, his hands roam to her hips, but instead of touching for pleasure, he begins to guide her hips in their swaying. He motions her hips so that they are in perfect rhythm with the music. When she seems to feel the pulse,* **EFREN** *moves back, letting her dance on her own. She holds the beat for a few steps; a smile breaks across her face. However when the music changes tempo,* **ADRAY** *falters, she tries to catch up, but almost trips over her own feet. She stops, opening her eyes embarrassed.* **MARIACHI** *keeps playing, inviting her to try again.*

ADRAY. *(to* **MARIACHI GUITAR PLAYER**) Alright, alright.

(music ceases)

Please...please can you just...

(She dismisses him. **MARIACHI GUITAR PLAYER** *disappointedly slides his guitar on his back and nods to* **ADRAY** *pleasantly.* **ADRAY** *instinctively reaches for money, but realizes she threw her wallet at* **EFREN** *earlier. She apologizes.* **MARIACHI GUITAR PLAYER** *begins to exit, but then he stops. He looks back at* **ADRAY**.*)

MARIACHI GUITAR PLAYER. You know what? No. I don't feel like goin'. I just played my heart out, I just played for you a song I wrote especial for my little one, and you ask me to go like some waiter who is in your face every five seconds? Like some motherfucker just trying to earn a tip...?

ADRAY. I'm sorry, I—

MARIACHI GUITAR PLAYER. You know how come you can't hear mi música?

ADRAY. ...

MARIACHI GUITAR PLAYER. 'Cuz I'm a joke to you.

ADRAY. He has my wallet.

MARIACHI GUITAR PLAYER. Repita por favor???

(**ADRAY** *looks to* **EFREN**)

EFREN. Hey, this between you an'—

MARIACHI GUITAR PLAYER. "He has your wallet?" An' what does that mean, Señorita?

ADRAY. *(to* **EFREN***)* Can you please give me my—

(**EFREN** *tosses the wallet between* **ADRAY** *and* **MARIACHI GUITAR PLAYER**, *they both look down at it*)

MARIACHI GUITAR PLAYER. You know something, if that is how you see things between us, señorita; if you see us that we can be only just jokes to each other, then what can I do?

(**MARIACHI GUITAR PLAYER** *picks up the wallet.*)

ADRAY. I'm sorry, I don't know what you're—

MARIACHI GUITAR PLAYER. Señorita, señorita, por favor. Do I have the permissions to talk?

ADRAY. Yes.

MARIACHI GUITAR PLAYER. You see, I tried to make you beautiful. I tried show you what my love sound like. But I don't haffta do that. See:

(**MARIACHI GUITAR PLAYER** *begins the intro to* "***LA BAMBA****,*" *then quickly bows, removing his sombrero and dumping her entire contents of her wallet inside it before placing it back on his head.*)

I only hope for two things the next time we are close to each other. First, that you get smaller shoes. Those are too big for you, y'know. No wonder you trip all over yourself.

ADRAY. And?

MARIACHI GUITAR PLAYER. Ehh?

ADRAY. The second thing you hope for.

MARIACHI GUITAR PLAYER. That you won't give up on things so easy.

(MARIACHI GUITAR PLAYER exits strumming the ballad he had previously been playing.)

Adios señorita!

(The music drowns away. ADRAY picks up her emptied wallet, she looks up at EFREN embarrassed. Lights spill to VIVIA and JUANA sitting on either side of JONAH.)

VIVIA. Eh…Mister Jonah, can I get for you something else, something else to help you enjoy…

JONAH. …something else…?

VIVIA. Sí.

(VIVIA whispers into JONAH's ear, his attention raises. JUANA looks away disappointed.)

JONAH. You…you can get that?

VIVIA. For you, sí.

JONAH. How much?

VIVIA. Cheaper than you ever paid and more than you ever had.

JONAH. Two-for-one?

VIVIA. Not for this.

JONAH. How would we, I mean do, where do we—

VIVIA. You just have to come with me just over there a little ways.

(JONAH looks to JUANA.)

JUANA. Don't look at me, this between you an'—

JONAH. But is it—

JUANA. Safe?

VIVIA. Don't worry, Mister Jonah, I be right next to you like the whole time. Come...

(**JONAH** *takes a few moments, but then allows* **VIVIA** *to lead him away from the bar.* **JUANA** *watches him go. Then looks around at the bar with wonder and nerves. She speaks across borders...*)

JUANA. Hey mijo, I hope that everything okay for you today. I know es exciting to find someone. I remember. An… if white's the way you like'em, white's how I'm gonna like'em too. *(pause)* Just make sure that she treat you all-the-time-good, no matter how things get, that she always on your side of things, mijo. *(pause)* An' hey, whatever happen, I'm glad you got yourself a little somebody to be with. Even if she a güera, I'm real glad.

(**JUANA** *puts her mouth for another sip, then doesn't like the taste. Lights shift to* **VIVIA** *and* **JONAH** *standing across from* **MEXICAN DRUG DEALER**, *played by same actor as* **MARIACHI**, *counting American dollar bills, when he is done he blatantly tosses a tiny, packed plastic rectangle of off-white.* **JONAH** *doesn't catch it and worriedly drops to the floor to scoop it up.*)

MEXICAN DRUG DEALER. Eh, maricón, ain't you play beisbol?

JONAH. No I...

(**JONAH** *studies the bag conspicuously.*)

...never played...

MEXICAN DRUG DEALER. Hey, maricón, it's no shit you never played, you can't catch for shit.

(to **VIVIA***)* Hey Vivia, where you find this maricón?

(**VIVIA** *shrugs.*)

What, you don' know?

(**JONAH** *opens the bag, dots his finger, tastes.*)

You bring some maricón who can't play beisbol to me an' you don'even know if you found him in the drunk tank or in the lobby Camino Real?

VIVIA. I think he one uh the ones stuck from the red buses.

MEXICAN DRUG DEALER. Que?

VIVIA. Los autobuses rojo. Mexicoach.

MEXICAN DRUG DEALER. I understand what red means, Vivia. What about them?

VIVIA. The buses, they all broke down this morning. So en la Revolución all los turistas are stuck. They don't know what to do, stay or go.

JONAH. We didn't—we weren't on any of the red buses.

MEXICAN DRUG DEALER. 'Scuse me?

JONAH. I'm just saying, my wife an' I, we weren't on the red buses, that's all.

MEXICAN DRUG DEALER. So you don't play beisbol, you weren't on the red buses. Wow. Maricón, you sound like a fas'cin'ating motherfucker.

(beat)

JONAH. Um...

MEXICAN DRUG DEALER. *(to VIVIA)* What did he say?

VIVIA. I think he said "Um."

(JONAH holds up the packed plastic.)

JONAH. There's like...specks.

MEXICAN DRUG DEALER. Specks?

JONAH. The color, see? It doesn't look...pure.

MEXICAN DRUG DEALER. So, Vivia, if you didn't find him from the buses, where did you find him then?

VIVIA. ...I think I found him in a bar, I think.

MEXICAN DRUG DEALER. Is he drunk?

JONAH. It's just...kinda a lot of money is all.

MEXICAN DRUG DEALER. Maricón, where you from?

JONAH. The States.

MEXICAN DRUG DEALER. You sure?

JONAH. Um, yea.

MEXICAN DRUG DEALER. Like one-hundred percent?

JONAH. Positive, why?

MEXICAN DRUG DEALER. 'Cuz I don' know what it is, but something about you, maricón, look like you live right close to here, that you are here all the time, maybe San Diego, maybe—

JONAH. No, I'm north of Los Angeles actually, by—

(MEXICAN DRUG DEALER excites, he nudges VIVIA)

What...?

MEXICAN DRUG DEALER. So...do you know where like is Santa Clarita, California?

JONAH. Yea, that's *exactly* where I—well no, not exactly, but—

MEXICAN DRUG DEALER. Is it like complicated to get to?

JONAH. ...not really.

(They both stare at JONAH.)

...you'd just go up the 5.

MEXICAN DRUG DEALER. Tha's it?

JONAH. Why are you asking?

MEXICAN DRUG DEALER. Vivia here has a little vacación of her own coming soon. Eh, "coming soon," that sounds like how in the movies, huh? "Coming soon...*Vivia's Vacation*, starring..." well fuck, starring Vivia I guess, huh?

(MEXICAN DRUG DEALER pulls a small, clean photograph. He shows it to JONAH.)

See, lookit that, maricón, tha's like the brochure I give to her. Take it.

(JONAH takes the photo, glances at it unimpressed.)

Like a dream, huh? Tha's what's called a "dream house," no?

JONAH. I guess.

MEXICAN DRUG DEALER. Not you guess, es a dreamhouse or es not?

JONAH. Yes. It's...very dreamy.

MEXICAN DRUG DEALER. Give it to her.

JONAH. Give what?

MEXICAN DRUG DEALER. The dream house? I want you to give it to Vivia. Por favor.

(JONAH hands VIVIA the photograph, she looks at it and cannot help but smile like she hasn't in years.)

Now, I want you to give to her direction.

JONAH. ...you still just take the 5. Northbound.

VIVIA. The 5 to the north'bound, si.

MEXICAN DRUG DEALER. Tell her how easy.

JONAH. It's not hard.

VIVIA. I'm not so uh good behind the wheel, you know.

JONAH. ...just stay in your lane, honk the horn if anybody gets too close. And just...ride all the way up. Really it's not that hard, I think...I don't know you, but I imagine you could...get there.

VIVIA. Thank you, my gentle'man.

MEXICAN DRUG DEALER. Y'know, you could be like a pretty good travel agent, same as me. Maricón the Dreamy, Gentle Travelman.

JONAH. Thank you.

MEXICAN DRUG DEALER. I'm gonna make with you a deal, ehh.

JONAH. I'm actually fine, with the specks. I'm sorry that I...I don't need—

MEXICAN DRUG DEALER. See I'm a hard worker, maricón; I got three jobs. I deal in...specks, according to you.

JONAH. No, I didn't mean—

MEXICAN DRUG DEALER. Then there's the travel agenting. An...I don't like to float my own boat, is that how you say? Float my own boat?

JONAH. ...yes.

MEXICAN DRUG DEALER. But…I dance. Yea. My body is like an instrument. You know, nothing fancy, just for pleasure's sake.

JONAH. That's great.

MEXICAN DRUG DEALER. But I don't do that for the money. If people give me money, okay, but I move because my heart wants me to.

JONAH. …I'd love to watch you sometime.

MEXICAN DRUG DEALER. Yea?

JONAH. Yea.

MEXICAN DRUG DEALER. No.

(VIVIA *laughs nervously.*)

But with my other two jobs, I want to be the best that I can be with them. Do you know?

JONAH. Of course.

MEXICAN DRUG DEALER. So I make a promise to you right now, mister dreamy gentle maricón man, that I'm gonna get you that pure like you said for. No specks.

JONAH. I don't need pure, really, I probably can't even tell the difference—

MEXICAN DRUG DEALER. Hey, Dreamy'man. I want to.

JONAH. I appreciate that, but actually—

MEXICAN DRUG DEALER. As a matter of fact, Vivia here is going to help me get it.

VIVIA. I am the one going to…make it happen.

MEXICAN DRUG DEALER. See, maricón, right now you inspire me. All this time I been giving to people specks an' I didn't even know it. Nobody ever complain before.

JONAH. Vivia, y'know what, maybe this was—can we cancel or—

MEXICAN DRUG DEALER. I look up to you. Your dreamy business sense. See I'm not like all those other lazy Mejicanos. They all talk. Me, I do. Vivia, do. Thanks to you. Ha, see I rhyme too.

JONAH. …

MEXICAN DRUG DEALER. Mi Vivia here is gonna take like a little vacación a California. Al norte de Los Ángeles. An' do you know how come?

JONAH. No.

MEXICAN DRUG DEALER. Because I don't want you to think I'm some kinda joke, selling specks an' filthy shit. I'm movin' up. Like the Jeffersons. *(pause)* You know, on the T.V. *(pause)* Vivia, maricón-man don't know what I'm talking about, sing for him the Jeffersons.

VIVIA. *(singing)* We're movin' on up—

JONAH. I know the song, I know the Jeffersons.

MEXICAN DRUG DEALER. So wha's the next line then? *(pause)* Go on, say it to me.

JONAH. …we're movin' on up, to the east side. To a deluxe apartment in the sky…

MEXICAN DRUG DEALER. Ay, maricón, you know what your voice sound like?

JONAH. No.

MEXICAN DRUG DEALER. Es dreamy. When you sung about "up in the sky"…I like felt it. Didn't you feel it, Vivia?

VIVIA. A little.

(MEXICAN DRUG DEALER hands VIVIA a set of keys and a manila envelope.)

MEXICAN DRUG DEALER. So go on then, Vivia, we've a customer waiting.

JONAH. Wait. Vivia, don't—

(VIVIA takes the keys and envelope downstage. Lights shift to her. We are at an embankment of the Tijuana River. It is quiet. VIVIA dusts herself off. JONAH and MEXICAN DRUG DEALER watch.)

VIVIA. *(to audience)* Well…he was never much of an agent. All the times, he just only always talk about how much a wonderful thing this one, especial vacation will be, 'specially for a new mother like me. An' when I try to ask if he got any other trips to take…he don't. What kinda travel agent only have one place to go?

(to **MEXICAN DRUG DEALER***)* You say it to me that it was a one in a million trip. One in a million. An' si, I like how that sound coming from my mouth. I never have a million of nothing. 'Cept nosebleeds. I bet you that's where I take the queen, bleeding from my nose.

(to audience) An' you know something, right when he's talking at me, my nose went bleeding. Yea, just like that. So he give me a torn page from *El Sol de Tijuana* to stop it up. An' then he say to me a promise that all my bleeding will come to an end, if I take this one little trip.

A California. Al norte de Los Ángeles.

Me, I don't believe in him at first. I know in my head I think about waking up in California all the time. I also know it ain't so easy as that. But I like what the nice gentle'man say to me, that I can get there.

So I believe.

I believe that a for reals Jeep Cherokee will be waiting for me an' that this keys will work. I believe about these papers will have my foto an' name. And I even believe how I'll roll my window down para La Migra and smile my eyes as I cross La Linea so easy. Speeding up the engine as I go up into the fat freeways what I seen on T.V.

An' me, I will drive through Los Ángeles, nobody noticing me for anything but that I belong. Maybe I'll even make my horn go if another car get too close. For truth, I don't know why people make their horns go, it don't do nothing, but me/I'd like to try. Ha. Wouldn't that be something, huh? Me making like I got a right to something. Like I got a say. Making my horn go all the way north the 5 freeway to that house in Santa Clarita, just like the gentle'man tell me to do. I still got the foto, see…

(VIVIA drops the keys and envelope, pulling a crushed, soiled photo from her person.)

This is where I was gonna stay till I earn enough to bring over my baby. Felix. See, got a yard an' upstairs too. An' I can't really see it in the foto, but says there's a pool out back. With a view outlooking to some amusement park. Magicland or something likeso, I don't remember.

I'm gonna keep this foto with me. I know es stupid. I know I got no use. But I don't care, lookit me…

(She looks back towards river.)

…I could use something nice to look at, huh? Even if it ain't so true.

(beat)

Now, I don't know much for Jeep Cherokee; sure the engine sound okay, the license plate read California, just like he say…but it look used inside, all taped up. And this is I am thinking when a grey, Chevy van cuts me off. *(pause)* My hand to the horn…but it don't even make a sound. I should've asked for a Toyota.

Two of the men go after my tires, an' one stands by my window, staring at me like he bored. Oh, an' they all got machine guns. I think this is a thing-to-know, if you're telling a story about your dream vacación and it involves machine guns, you probably had not so good a travel agent.

They don't even keep the Cherokee. They just rip from my tires three packages wrapped in rubber and invite me with ugly mouths to get into the Chevy.

They tell me we are going for a swim. But they don't look at me in my eyes when then say this to me, no all six of their looks are looking at different parts of me. So I don't really believe in them.

My travel agent, he used to tell me I will be laying on la playa, watching the clean California water con mi Felix one day. But while I'm laying on the side of this river, on my back, waiting for all six, one by one... *(pause)* I look at the water and all I can think is how it don't look so clean. The water I lay next to is shit. I wouldn't want mi Felix here, anywhere close. An' I feel so stupid for letting him down.

(beat)

This morning, they found two men from la policía without their heads along this same river. So I'm not so much surprised when I see one of the men put down his machine gun an' pick up a machete instead.

An' d'you know something?...I could still see. Even after he bring the machete down on my neck, for some little bit of seconds, I could still see as they kicked my body towards water.

It's not an unthinkable amount of kilometers between that pole I tried to make money for mi Felix in Tijuana and that fotographic house in Santa Clarita. Magicland. Was just a Cherokee ride away.

*(She looks back at **JONAH**, who cannot face her.)*

An I can't help but laugh at myself how close it seem, talking to this one gentle'man. Hearing him tell me how easy. All such shit telling me that I can get there. Be there.

But lookit me, smiling maybe, but my nose is probably bleeding again. It just doesn't need stopping up 'cuz, well...my body ain't so much attached, y'know.

But I know my heart will do that. Keep pumping blood, even if it has no place to go. I don't think you can blame a heart for that. It has no idea how far things are. Always they seem so close.

(*VIVIA exits. Alone onstage is* **JONAH** *and* **MEXICAN DRUG DEALER,** *who reaches out for* **JONAH**'s *hand and shakes it firmly.* **JONAH** *pulls his hand away, a little hurt.* **MEXICAN DRUG DEALER** *exits, leaving* **JONAH** *alone onstage. Lights out on Act One.*)

ACT TWO

(JUANA *and* EFREN *stand at the mouth of the alley,* ADRAY *and* JONAH *in the background.* EFREN *downs a Gallo wine.*)

JUANA. *(across borders)* Hey there, mijo, lookit you.

(to EFREN*)* Oh, lookit him, Efren.

(across borders) I love when you put that smile, mijo, so handsome. I wish it you would put it more, but I know, I remember. Sometimes everything feels like you don't wanna smile, but when you find a reason...es like es all you can do.

(to EFREN*)* Lookit him, Efren, lookit how he dressed so fit. Tucked his shirt an' everything.

(across borders) An' tha's how you haffta do, mijo, even if it don't feel like you, even if it feel like the clothes they don't really fit. You haffta try. So when the people there see you, they see that you fit just fine. You can fit anywhere, mijo, anywhere you wanna be you can fit into. My promise to you, huh. The most perfect shape you are, mijo. Just the most perfect...

(beat)

(to EFREN*)* I'm worried, Efren.

EFREN. No...

JUANA. That Angelita say she like him okay, but—

EFREN. What is?

JUANA. What if I don't recognize him, Efren, what if now he gonna fit so many new places that when we see him again *(She signs the cross.)* what if he don't look like our boy no more. I don't want his shape to change, Efren.

EFREN. He'll be okay.

JUANA. How can you say that, *these people...*

EFREN. I know.

JUANA. If this is how they raised their Angelita...

(switch to **ADRAY** *and* **JONAH***)*

ADRAY. They don't want our money.

JONAH. I know.

ADRAY. What's wrong?

JONAH. She had a kid. Felix.

ADRAY. Who had a kid? Who the hell is Felix?

JONAH. No one, never mind. Look we have to get out of here.

(switch)

EFREN. Juana. No matter how we raised Javi, he better than me. Maybe even better than you.

JUANA. You think their Angela, that she better than—

EFREN. Hey. Salud. To our little shit...an' his güerita.

*(***EFREN** *toasts with his bottle, then pulls back. When he is done, he thumps his chest, trying to help himself breathe.)*

JUANA. ¿Que paso?

EFREN. Got that shit crawlin' up real bad today, Fea. I can feel it snaking up my pipes, stickin' its acid wet tongue, beggin' ta get out.

JUANA. It's more than before, huh?

(switch)

JONAH. They mentioned Santa Clarita.

ADRAY. What?

JONAH. Adray, what if they know where we live.

ADRAY. Our address is on my driver's license.

(switch)

EFREN. I try ta drown him, Juana. But snake won't let me. See feel right here, put your hand. You can feel it in my chest slivering up.

(EFREN *tries to put* JUANA*'s hand; she pulls away.*)

JUANA. I don't like it sliverin'up.

(*switch*)

ADRAY. Jonah, did Juana mention Angela?

(JONAH *nods.*)

JONAH. Have you talked to her?

(ADRAY *nods.*)

Is she okay? Wha'd she say, did you tell her anything?

ADRAY. ...no. She seemed fine. But...

JONAH. What?

ADRAY. You don't think that...maybe Efren and Juana are distracting us meanwhile somebody else is like...going towards Angela?

(*switch*)

JUANA. You jus'be strong, Efren. For Javi. I ain't having no snake even close to where he—

EFREN. ...way down from almost where my piss holds, all the way up to where I'm talkin'too loud with. Tha's almost two feet long this snake is. But I can hold him down there, Fea. For you. For Javi. An' if ever it tries to sneak out, then I bite down hard an' guess what's for dinner?

JUANA. What is?

EFREN. Snake soup.

(*switch*)

ADRAY. What if Javier isn't even their son, what if he's some guy who's got our address and knows Angela is home alone. You even fucking said to Juana she's home. Alone.

JONAH. Why would they do that? Why would they go through *all* this trouble, drive *all* that way. We're middle class.

(switch)

JUANA. Hey Efren.

EFREN. Yea, Juanita?

JUANA. I'm scared for Javi to be open like this. His little heart, his little mouth, his little everything.

EFREN. He'll be okay, Juana.

JUANA. What if all this time though, he was at least safe. But now with this little güerita let inside, what if other things sneak inside too.

*(**EFREN** and **JUANA** turn back towards the belly of the alleyway. They watch **JONAH** and **ADRAY**.)*

ADRAY. Jones... *(pause)* I asked Angela what the name of that boy she's in love with is.

She said his name is Javier.

JONAH. Juana told me the same thing.

ADRAY. What the fuck is this, Jonah?

JONAH. We'll find a phone, we'll call Angela, tell her go to next door and stay with them till we get home.

ADRAY. Are they even home?

JONAH. Then call the police, tell them...tell them there's a student at Dos Pueblos in Angela's year, an' that his name is Javier and he's been harassing her. Threatening her. Tell them that whatever Javier is enrolled at Dos Pueblos needs to be picked up.

ADRAY. An' if there's not a Javier enrolled there?

JONAH. Tell Angela to stay at the neighbors' till we come get her, tell her I don't want her going home. For anything.

ADRAY. You think our neighbors' is safe?

JONAH. Well I don't know where—

ADRAY. Maybe Angela should just go to the police straight. Maybe she should go to them and just say that there's a kid or man named Javier who might be trying to hurt her.

JONAH. A man named Javier. That's gonna scare the shit out of her.

ADRAY. Well, what else can we do?

JONAH. Tell the police to just pick up all the Javiers in the entire city and hold them till she's back with us.

ADRAY. Just lock the entire city down a city, all of it.

JONAH. Then pull everybody over, check their ID an' if it says anything resembling Javier, hold 'em till every parent is safe and with their kids.

ADRAY. We still don't have a phone, Jonah.

(ADRAY and JONAH hold each other. Lights move to JUANA and EFREN.)

JUANA. Do you see? Do you see the way they talk about him.

EFREN. Don't you worry, Javi ain't done nothing—

JUANA. They're calling my boy a harassing. A threatner. That he needs to be picked up.

EFREN. Nobody's pickin' him up, Fea.

JUANA. Don't call me that.

EFREN. Hey, que pasa?

JUANA. If some Americano say he need to be picked up, Efren, he will be.

EFREN. How they gonna call, huh? There's only one phone an' I got it.

(JUANA dials the phone, immediate voicemail, she hangs up.)

He not answering?

(shakes her head)

JUANA. What if something wrong, Efren?

EFREN. Or maybe he just not answering. Cálmate, Juanita.

(JUANA looks to JONAH and ADRAY.)

JUANA. Lookit them. What kinda parents don't carry with them their phones, huh?

EFREN. Hey, we already searched them, huh.

JUANA. They prolly got super small ones, can't even feel it over their clothes.

EFREN. Juana, if they had a way to call, they would've.

JUANA. You promise to me, Efren, that our Javi will be okay for reals. *Nothing* will happen to him.

EFREN. Te lo prometo.

(EFREN and JUANA walk to JONAH and ADRAY. EFREN pulls his mobile phone and puts it in front of ADRAY.)

(to ADRAY) Dial your daughter. Por favor.

ADRAY. I already did earlier.

EFREN. I ain't asking earlier. I'm asking now.

JONAH. Has something happened?

JUANA. Three times a day, no?

ADRAY. Why're you—

(EFREN puts the phone aggressively in ADRAY's face.)

JONAH. Hey!

(ADRAY takes her time in grabbing the phone. She pulls the calling card; EFREN takes the card from her and tosses it.)

EFREN. I'll accept your charges, güera.

(ADRAY touches the phone keypad causing lights to turn young again. EFREN and ADRAY look at each other like teenagers; they speak that way too.)

"Missed you."

ADRAY. "All day I been looking. I was looking for you at lunch."

EFREN. "I had to stay in Cooking."

ADRAY. "What happened?"

EFREN. "I dunno. The substitute said she needed me to stay in the room for a while. Like that I stole something. I didn't, but that's what she acted like. So I was in there helping her wipe the countertops. But then know what I did?"

ADRAY. "What?"

EFREN. "I tol' to her that I didn't steal nada. And that I shouldn've have let her keep me in her kitchen for during my free time. I said that I can't be inside like that 'cuz ..."

ADRAY. "'Cuz why?"

EFREN. "'Cuz I got somebody waiting for me now, an' I'm not gonna let some stupid whatever-this-is keep me from you, Angela."

ADRAY. "You told her that, you said my name?"

EFREN. "That's all I been doing since earlier. Saying your name. Feeling it in my mouth. Angela."

ADRAY. "So she knows...she knows that we...that me an' you are like..."

EFREN. "Don't you want people to know?"

ADRAY. "Yes. I do. Omigod, I wonder what they'll think."

(She laughs.)

EFREN. "What's so funny?"

ADRAY. "Um...my parents aren't home."

EFREN. "Till when?"

ADRAY. "Supposed to be late tonight, but they always stay an extra day when they go places, always telling me how there's just one more something my mom just has to see, then they'll be back first thing."

EFREN. "My parents would never do that. I gotta call 'em like all the time."

ADRAY. "They're strict?"

EFREN. "Nah, they just worry."

ADRAY. "So...you wanna come home with me, Javier?"

(He nods eagerly.)

EFREN. "So, what? You wanna walk out together, in front of everybody, right through the…"

ADRAY. "Yea, right where everyone can see, straight through the yard, to the north fence."

EFREN. "But everybody hangs out back there."

ADRAY. "I know. I never go out that way. But now I got you."

(They walk across through sounds of gossiping school children, holding each other's hands tight as they do. Proud. After a few moments though, they come to a stop.)

EFREN. "Hey, uh…why don't we just go back the other way, c'mon."

ADRAY. "No. Everyday everybody makes me nervous, but not today."

EFREN. "We'll go this way tomorrow."

ADRAY. "If we walk like we're one person, nobody will be able to say anything."

EFREN. "Promise?"

(ADRAY looks into EFREN's eyes and kisses him. For a few moments it is beautiful. Like they have been meaning to kiss for generations. But soon a few teenage catcalls can be heard. EFREN stops the kiss and holds ADRAY's hand tight as he looks offstage with handmade confidence.)

ADRAY. *(to offstage)* "Why don't you just leave us alone?"

EFREN. "Let's just go."

ADRAY. *(to offstage)* "So what if that's his name. We've got just as much right to come through this fence as you do."

EFREN. "Angela, c'mon, c'mon we can go back—"

(They stop holding hands. The lights dim rather quickly. In the darkness…)

ADRAY. *(to offstage)* "Look I don't even know what you're talking about. Who cares if he's a Javier. Why don't you just leave him alone! Leave him alone!"

(Lights grow old quickly; ADRAY hangs up the phone slowly. They speak as adults again.)

JUANA. Oh, mi Javi...

JONAH. *(to JUANA)* I'm sorry.

ADRAY. Me too.

JUANA. Efren, me lo prometiste.

EFREN. Lo siento, mi amor.

(JUANA begins messing with the machine gun, trying to find a safety switch.)

EFREN. Juanita.

JUANA. After thirteen years of my perfect boy, now look at him. He gets called what, names at the school. They never bother him before. He tries to make it with her through a fence at a schoolyard an' they won't even let him do that.

JONAH. Maybe he's fine though, Juana.

JUANA. My boy is attacked today and you two look at me? Giving apologies to me?

ADRAY. Efren, we're sorry for what happened.

JUANA. Not Efren, estupida! What have you to say to mi Javier? Huh?

JONAH. We wish that none of this had happened. Any of it.

JUANA. What about you, puta?

ADRAY. The same.

JUANA. Would you call for him to be locked up? Huh?

ADRAY. ...

JUANA. No, you don't be silent with me, puta. You answer me what I'm asking.

ADRAY. What do you want me to say?

JONAH. We wouldn't do anything like that to him, we're not like that.

EFREN. You never even met my boy, you never even care to know what he look like and you would have him locked up.

JONAH. No, I'm sorry, but no we wouldn't have him locked up, we would *never* have *anyone's* child—

JUANA. But did you *want* to? *(pause)* Did you want my boy an' anybody resembling my boy to be locked up, güero? ¡Dime!

JONAH. …yes, but…but we didn't mean it. We were…angry. Scared that…Angela might be…

EFREN. Be what?

JONAH. In danger.

JUANA. From who?

JONAH. I…I don't know.

JUANA. You make yourself scared of mi Javier, then what chance does he have. Huh?

JONAH. Look, I don't know exactly, we were just scared for her and so we might've…

EFREN. What.

JONAH. We just didn't want to take any chances.

JUANA. Mi Javi isn't a harasser, he isn't anything bad unless you make him that way!

JONAH. We let our imaginations go a bit, that's all.

JUANA. Say it.

JONAH. He isn't anything bad.

JUANA. *(to ADRAY)* An' now you, Little Thing.

ADRAY. Me, what?

JUANA. I want you to say that mi Javier is an honest boy. That he kind. And that he wouldn't hurt your Angela not ever.

ADRAY. What does it matter what I say?

JUANA. Say it.

ADRAY. What is that gonna do, me saying that I—

JONAH. Adray, what is the *matter* with you?

ADRAY. It doesn't matter what I say, Jonah.

JONAH. If it doesn't matter then just fucking say what they want.

ADRAY. Me saying something isn't going to make it happen.

EFREN. What would you say then, Little Thing, to make happen?

JUANA. You say it to me now, that mi Javier is okay next to your Angela or—

(JUANA *nudges the gun towards* **JONAH**.)

JONAH. Adray, Jesus Christ!

EFREN. Juana, calmaté.

ADRAY. You want us to be honest. Right. *(pause)* Well, I don't want your Javier next to our Angela. I just do not. And I can't help if that's how I feel. She's our daughter, not yours.

(JUANA *puts the gun at* **JONAH**'s *chest*.)

JONAH. Adray!

JUANA. I tol' you there's only one reason for a gun to be unsafety.

ADRAY. Juana, if you do *anything* to him, my Angela will break your Javi's heart in fucking two.

EFREN. ...the hell're you talkin'?

ADRAY. You said it yourself, they're in love right.

JUANA. Dile que pare, Efren, no me gusta.

ADRAY. I imagine she's right beside him in that hospital, y'know, just the way a girlfriend knows how to. His scared hand cradled in her perfect little paw, oh their paws an' mittens are mixed-up as fuck. But, Juana, Efren, the moment you put this Tijuana alleyway to unsafety, my Angela is gonna dig her manicured nails right past your boy's unsuspecting mitten into his trembling fucking paw.

And the police will come. And who do you think they'll believe in? Oh, they'll drag him in for being a harasser. They'll yell an' scream ugly things at him, an' why he'll barely even be able to acknowledge to the police that he's ready to sign his name across that confession they've been putting in front of him for several hours.

But he will. He'll write his name in that ugly cursive that teenage boys do, that he, Javier, is a threat to the U.S. nation.

See, I don't care how guilty you want us. I've raised my Angela to protect herself.

(*across borders*) Ain't that right, baby? If that Javier gets up too close, you get away from him any way you can think to. And then you call the police, even if you have to scream it from the streets.

(*The lights sputter for a moment before turning over to* **JAVIER** *and* **ANGELA**, *played by the actors who played* **VIVIA** *and* **MARIACHI/DRUG DEALER**. **JAVIER** *sleeps in a hospital bed.*)

ANGELA. Hey…hey…is that you waking up, Javi? Can you hear me?

JAVIER. Is that you?

ANGELA. Yea, it's me.

JAVIER. Where am I? Are we…is this your parents' house?

ANGELA. No. This is a hospital.

JAVIER. How long…

ANGELA. Not long.

JAVIER. Am I gonna be alright?

ANGELA. Just keep drinking water. Try not to move.

JAVIER. My body hurts.

ANGELA. You've already got drugs in you to help the pain.

JAVIER. Thank you for staying.

(*beat*)

ANGELA. Javier, I've never really had a boyfriend before.

JAVIER. Boyfriend?

ANGELA. I know it was only a day, but that's as close to boyfriend as I've ever…

JAVIER. Angela, you're the first girl I ever…I never even thought anyone would ever—

ANGELA. So I don't know how I'm supposed to do things, and I'm probably gonna mess this up.

JAVIER. Hey, you can't mess up with me.

ANGELA. Thank you for saying that. So this probably isn't the most ideal way to do this, but...I don't know if we're gonna work out.

JAVIER. Wait, wha—

ANGELA. I know, I know, maybe I'm supposed to wait to do this sorta thing, but I dunno, I just...if I wait, it's just gonna be that much harder to do, won't it?

JAVIER. Angela. Why're you...what is this?

ANGELA. So I just think...let's just get on with our childhoods, ya know?

JAVIER. I can be stronger. For you I can be stronger. I can be. Please just let me—

ANGELA. Coming through that fence with you, Javi—I didn't feel safe...like I imagined I would. I thought the two of us side by side, we shoulda been *so* strong. What possible danger could there be? To you an' me. To love.

JAVIER. I do, you know. Love you.

ANGELA. Javi, you're so sweet. You are. But by that fence, in front of everyone, was like you were a joke. *(pause)* When they was laughing at you on the...oh, I'm so sorry to say this, but some weird tiny part of me almost wanted to laugh with them. Just to be safe. An' I know this isn't probably the best time to tell this to you, but...I could feel we weren't meant for each other before they...crashed across your face.

(JAVIER *looks away. He reaches out for the call button.*)

I don't think it works, Javier. I was pressing it earlier when you were still out. Just to see what would happen. Know what's funny? It feels good to press. Even if it don't go nowhere.

JAVIER. Why did you make us go through there?

ANGELA. What?

JAVIER. The fence.

ANGELA. I should go.

JAVIER. No, I'm sorry, I'm sorry, please don't leave me here by my—

ANGELA. I want a boy to make me feel safe.

JAVIER. Wait, what if I need—this button it doesn't—I need help.

ANGELA. I have to be home.

JAVIER. Ayúdame, por favor

ANGELA. Ayúdame?

JAVIER. It means help.

ANGELA. You see, Javier, even here by your hospital bed, hearing you talk, I know we aren't right for being next to one another.

(ANGELA moves to exit, then stops herself.)

Thank you for the beautiful we shared this morning, I'll replay it in my thoughts often.

(ANGELA exits.)

JAVIER. ¡Mamá! ¡Papá! ¡Ayúdame! ¡Por Favor!

(Lights begin to dim.)

JUANA. *(across borders to* **JAVIER***)* ¡Javi!

JONAH. *(across borders to* **ANGELA***)* Angela!
What happened to you, Angie? Why…why would you be like that?

ANGELA. *(across borders to* **ADRAY** *and* **JONAH***)* Sorry. I thought that was what you guys wanted.

(ANGELA exits. A moment. Both couples stare at each other. **EFREN** *takes the machine gun from* **JUANA***; coughing, thumping his chest.)*

JUANA. Efren…

ADRAY. Think about what you're doing, Efren.

JONAH. Shut your mouth, Adray.

EFREN. Don't worry, mi Juanita, I bite him down for you, for Javi.

(**EFREN** *moves in on* **ADRAY** *and* **JONAH** *with the gun in his hands. It looks as though he is going to use the mass of it, do something with it, though not shoot.*)

JUANA. ¿Efren, que estas hacien—

ADRAY. The longer you hold that gun, the more that's who you are. It doesn't matter why he holds it, Juana. In fact, maybe one day Javier will pick up a machine gun too. 'Cuz that's who he'll be. And your family will never change.

An' I know you two don't want that. For your children and their children after. What parents would? So you can come at me with that unsafety machine gun, Efren, but just know what it is you're really doing.

JUANA. ¿Efren, qué haces?!

JONAH. Why don't we just, maybe put the gun down and take a moment...okay so your son needs help, he's scared, okay, so how can we help him? What can we do here to help Javier?

ADRAY. Who's gonna help *us*, Jonah? We haven't got anyone to help us either.

JONAH. I'm not talking about us, Adray! Now look, we can either keep on making this worse, or we can at least try to ease the situation. Juana, Efren—

(**EFREN** *throws the gun down at* **JONAH** *and* **ADRAY**'s *feet; they jump.*)

EFREN. See, I don't need a gun or anything to put the fear of México in you. 'Cuz right now, mi familia, is scared of *you*.

Mi Javier, all he wanted for was to have his'self a little girlfriend. Somebody to make him feel a little home in your California. Just someplace where he could maybe rest his head an' put his thoughts.

JUANA. An' you can't even let him do that.

EFREN. I know you two are scared too. But mi Javi, he didn't have nothing to do with that.

JONAH. Look, I apologize so completely to you both for... my God, for everything that's happened to—

ADRAY. No, no you're not going to stand there with a fucking machine gun on the floor and make my Jonah apologize to you. We didn't do fucking anything to you.

JUANA. You did more to us than you'll ever know, güera.

ADRAY. No, Jonah and me walked through that gate this morning and neither me or him had done one fucking thing to either you or your Javier. This morning, when you spotted us on La Revolución, there was nothing between us. Zero. An' now you say we hurt your perfect son, you say *you're* scared of *us.*
You Fucking Put A Gun To Our Faces. Is that what parents do here? No wonder this country is...

(JUANA *stares at* ADRAY, *who moves quick, and grabs the gun; she points it.*)

JONAH. Adray, what the fuck? You need to calm yourself and put the fucking gun down.

EFREN. *(to* ADRAY*)* Es not as heavy as mi Juanita said, huh? Easier to carry than people think. Es the picking it up tha's heavy.

JUANA. You make us do so many ugly things, just to get your serious attention.

JONAH. Don't do this. Look at yourself, Adray.

ADRAY. We don't have any choices, Jonah.

(ADRAY *begins to exit;* JONAH *does not follow.*)

JONAH. What, you wanna walk out there in the middle of Tijuana with a machine gun?
Adray, you're gonna get yourself shot.

EFREN. *(to* ADRAY*)* He's right, you know. If you do like this...

(ADRAY *points the gun at* EFREN *and* JUANA *as she exits.* JONAH *goes after her. She stops short. Enter* LA POLICÍA, *same actor as* MEXICAN DRUG DEALER. *He has a bloodied wrapped white cloth covering his neck. There is blood at his mouth, and bruises across his face.*)

LA POLICÍA. ¿Qué está pasando aqui?

JONAH. Oh, thank God. Please officer, there's been a horrible misunderstanding. This isn't…it's not what it looks like.

LA POLICÍA. Heh?

JONAH. *Please* help us, me an' my wife, we—

LA POLICÍA. You an' your wife? You mean your wife with the machine gun? Just you two need help? How about them? How'bout me?

EFREN. ¿Por qué está hablando chistoso?

LA POLICÍA. *(to* ADRAY/JONAH*)* You see, he ask how come I talk funny, but lookit him.

(to **EFREN***)* You got something inside you, huh? You look like you need to be spit up, huh?

(to **JUANA***)* Es that what he need, huh? Maybe a hand to his back an' a good cough, huh?

JUANA. ¿Estás bien? ¿Qué pasó?

(**LA POLICÍA** *grins, showing his teeth.*)

LA POLICÍA. When I wake up this, morning…guess wha'happen? *(pause)* Three of my teeth fall out. Ja. I felt they were okay last night, but today…

(**LA POLICÍA** *makes a whistling sound by breathing through his missing teeth.*)

Es like some fucked up tooth fairy came an' got me back for all the times I didn't leave her shit.

An d'you know something, these were mi amor's favorite too. Yea, these one, two, three, were her favorite teeth of mine. And now? They'll be buried in the dirt. Yea, mi amor, tha's what she'll react. Buried out in the garden, like they goin'grow back.

JONAH. Officer, please.

LA POLICÍA. Okay, okay, so uh what's uh goin'on here?

JONAH. That's not our gun. Adray, put the gun down.

ADRAY. I'm not putting anything.

JONAH. Adray, the police are here—

LA POLICÍA. Nah, es okay, you hold the gun for a little bit if it make you happy. You look ridiculous holding it anyways.

JONAH. Could you, we'd like to go to the station. Can we do that?

(**EFREN** and **LA POLICÍA** *laugh heavily.*)

LA POLICÍA. Quiere que lo lleven a la estación...eso es lo que dice.... Yea? Hey, okay, why don't you put those on then, huh?

(**LA POLICÍA** *tosses a pair of handcuffs to* **JONAH.**)

Go on, es one size fit all.

ADRAY. Jonah, don't you even think about—

JONAH. *(to* **LA POLICÍA**) What happens, sir, if I put these on?

LA POLICÍA. Wha' happens? *(pause)* Your hands'll be stuck together, puto, what you think happen?

ADRAY. Look, these two used this gun to force us into this alley. They've been holding us here and the only reason I have the gun is because we just want to go home. No charges. No reports. We just want to get out of here. Can you understand that? Can anyone understand that?

LA POLICÍA. Eh...señorita, may I say something?

ADRAY. No.

LA POLICÍA. If you eh...start walking, holding a machine gun like that, I'm gonna haffta...do my job.

ADRAY. Yes, fine, go on then, do your job!

LA POLICÍA. Perdon, but Señorita, you don't know for my job. You don't know what happen in my everyday, the things I go through. An' if you cannot be calm with the machine gun, Señorita, I'm going to have to ask you to put it down.

ADRAY. No doing.

LA POLICÍA. Why you no doing? Because I have the policía uniform on an' so you think that mean what? That I go crooked directions, ja? So many policía, they take the money an' they have so many snakebites all under their uniform. La Mordida. But, me, look:

(He rolls up his sleeves, shows his clean arms)

No snakebites. No bribes. Me, I think many times what if I just take a little extra pesos here, close my eyes a little there...but to be truth, I just don't want anything that bites near mi amor an' mi hijo. There are too many ugly things near our little house already.

ADRAY. Are you going to help us or aren't you? *(pause)* No? Jonah, let's go.

*(**ADRAY** begins walking.)*

JONAH. Adray, what are you doing?

ADRAY. This is how it works down here, they all work together. They probably planned this.

JONAH. You don't know that, Jesus Christ, you don't fucking know that.

LA POLICÍA. Ay, señorita, you see how you do. You gimme no choices.

*(**LA POLICÍA** unholsters. **ADRAY** points the gun upwards, looking as if to shoot.)*

JONAH. Adray, what the fuck?

ADRAY. Gunshots are loud, somebody will come.

JONAH. No, you're gonna get yourself in deeper an' then what, Adray? And then what? I go home alone? I go back home and tell Angela what? Look At Yourself, Please.

ADRAY. They're not gonna let us go, Jonah. They never were.

*(Pointing to the sky, **ADRAY** pulls the trigger. She flinches for the sound, but none comes. It clicks. Nothing. She tries again, but there are no fireworks. She shakes the gun. All look at her.)*

JONAH. ...Oh Jesus...Adray...how could you do that?

(**LA POLICÍA** *pulls his revolver, points it at* **ADRAY**.)

LA POLICÍA. *(to* **ADRAY***)* Pongase al suelo con sus manos detras de su cabeza, ahorita…

(**JONAH** *puts his hands up.*)

Your hands en su su cabeza, ahorita!

(**LA POLICÍA** *steers* **ADRAY** *to the floor, cuffing her hands behind her head. He looks to* **JONAH** *who quickly does it himself.*)

LA POLICÍA. Man, es too too hot for this shit. Sometimes I think how come for just some parts of the year, we an' Canada can't like switch places.

(**LA POLICÍA** *picks up the machine gun, shaking his head*)

(to **EFREN** *and* **JUANA***)* You know, you two are even estupider with a gun than her.

(**LA POLICÍA** *walks the machine gun over to* **ADRAY**.)

D'you see? It was on special. Right over in one of the shops. Many turistas bring this home to their sons. Because of how real it look, see.

(**LA POLICÍA** *then tosses the gun at* **EFREN** *and* **JUANA**.)

But this right here, for up close, c'mon you look.

(**LA POLICÍA** *puts his revolver in* **ADRAY** *and* **JONAH***'s face.*)

That is what real smell like.

JUANA. Señor policía—

LA POLICÍA. Ehh?

(**LA POLICÍA** *goes to* **EFREN** *and* **JUANA**.)

JUANA. They have a daughter.

LA POLICÍA. Lotsa people have daughters. Lotsa people have sons. What do you care? Lookit you.

EFREN. Señor Policía, por favor.

(LA POLICÍA looks at all four of them. He walks around the situation.)

LA POLICÍA. Listen up, ehh. I got something to say.

JUANA. Señor, por favor.

LA POLICÍA. That statement was like for all four of you.

EFREN. ¿Qué haces?

LA POLICÍA. So…a police officer walks into a…alleyway. An' he finds two Mejicanos and two Americanos. Oh, and a "machine gun" an' a lotta Tecates.

Shit, you guys need to drink better, that shit no good for you.

So…he say to the Mejicanos, "If you two were being held up in a different country, by what you thought was a fucking assault rifle, what would you have me do? *(pause)* Contéstame.

EFREN. …we want help.

JUANA. …yo tambien.

LA POLICÍA. Sí, you'd want me to do my fucking job. Like how I was trained to do. Wouldn't you? *(pause)* Wouldn't you?

(They respond. LA POLICÍA then turns to ADRAY and JONAH.)

(to ADRAY/JONAH) An' so the police officer says to the Americanos, "Tell me…if I come to *your* country, and raise what look like a machine gun to a police officer, what would happen to me? *(pause)* Well, say it to me, what would happen?"

JONAH. …you'd be arrested.

LA POLICÍA. I'd be shot, motherfucker. Like more than once. *(pause)* Those two maybe not so bright, but you two…you two are the luckiest people here today.

JONAH. Officer, we'd just like to get back to our daughter.

LA POLICÍA. So, what's stopping you?

JONAH. We…need the key.

LA POLICÍA. Señor, those are not those kind of handcuffs, if you truly want to go, they will let you.

(*JONAH and ADRAY try getting out of their cuffs. LA POLICÍA begins to laugh.*)

Tell me, back in America, is you two just always believe what somebody tell you. Of course you need the key, what kinda police officer walk around with handcuffs that don't lock?

(*LA POLICÍA drops a set of handcuff keys by them and looks at both couples.*)

You people, all of you, you believe too many things.

(*Enter VIVIA. All look at her. Dripping wet. She and LA POLICÍA look at each other.*)

(*to VIVIA*) Hello.

(*She responds.*)

Are you—

VIVIA. I know you. Seen you. Before. By the water.

LA POLICÍA. Me you too. By the water.

VIVIA. Where is your friend? The other one.

LA POLICÍA. …still by the river, I guess.

(*LA POLICÍA pulls the cloth from around his neck, revealing a severe slice encircling his neck. VIVIA feels her neck as well.*)

Our bodies, they found in Rosarito close to where a grade school is. To where children same age like mi hijo will be in the morning. We were wrapped. But not wrapped from respect for the dead. Los muertos. No, we were wrapped like presents. Just so only when they found us would it be revealed. Revealed that while our bodies lay wrapped in Rosarito, our heads would be found unwrapped someplace else. En el Río de Tijuana.

(*A luminescent blue over VIVIA and LA POLICÍA. Sounds of water. Both react.*)

VIVIA. En el Río de Tijuana.

LA POLICÍA. Where we understand each other that there was so many estupid forces for us to be by this horrible river. An' maybe you think it was your own bad mistakes made you end so awful. An' have no idea just how many kilometers deep an' ugly the ocean is that swallowed us both up an' then spit us out like that.

*(The blue begins to swallow **VIVIA** and **LA POLICÍA**.)*

An now all I can think of, es mi familia defenseless, in our little defenseless house, knowing that los policías is just as defenseless as them.

An today mi familia isn't safe, an' I was not strong enough to do anything about it.

*(The blue swallows **VIVIA** and **LA POLICÍA**. Lights back to the alley. A few moments, nobody talking, nobody looking at one another. A ringing is heard. **EFREN** pulls his mobile urgently. He answers.)*

EFREN. ¿¡Javi!? ¿¡Donde esta?! *(pause)* ¿Quien habla? *(pause)* Huh? *(pause)* Si, un momento, por favor.

*(**EFREN** looks to **JONAH**, hands him the phone.)*

Es for you.

JONAH. ...who is it?

EFREN. Take it.

*(**JONAH** does)*

JONAH. Uh...hello?

*(Lights reveal **ANGELA**, same actress as before, she sits in a clean, white, kitchen; she has been crying. Both couples watch.)*

ANGELA. Dad?

JONAH. ...Angie?

ANGELA. ....so, how's Mexico?

JONAH. Angela, what's a matter?

ANGELA. Is it fun?

JONAH. Angie, what is it?

ANGELA. Whose number is this anyways?

JONAH. Nevermind the number, Angela, what is it?

ANGELA. I'm in the kitchen. I was gonna get a snack. Hey, do you care if I finish your frozen little pocket things? There's not that many left.

JONAH. Stoppit.

ANGELA. I just…I had a really confusing day, you know.

JONAH. What happened?

ANGELA. So…this boy…

JONAH. Yea, I know.

ANGELA. …

JONAH. Angela, are you still there?

ANGELA. I thought I really really liked him. Like a lot. Like more than I ever… We…were like so…connected or something? You know?

JONAH. Yea. I do.

ANGELA. An' I thought that like, I could totally tell what I was feeling… But…I couldn't hold onto it. I wanted to hold onto it, but…it's like I wasn't strong enough. An' I keep feeling like it's all my fault, you know.

JONAH. It's not. Nothing, is your fault, Angie. Do you hear me? Not one thing is your fault.

ANGELA. You sound weird. Are you an' Mom okay?

JONAH. We're fine.

ANGELA. He was hurt, Dad. He was hurt real bad, an' I'm the one that did it.

JONAH. No, it's not you, you wouldn't hurt anyone—

(A doorbell, **ANGELA** *looks up towards it.)*

ANGELA. Wait, hold on, Daddy, somebody's at the door.

*(***ANGELA** *goes towards a door.)*

JONAH. No, Angela don't answer it.

(Before **ANGELA** *can open the door, there stands* **JAVIER**. *He looks exactly like somebody who fell in love in the*

morning, got the shit kicked out of them in the afternoon, and then had their heart broken not that long after.)

Angela, who is it, who's at the door.

JAVIER. ...

ANGELA. Javier, are you okay?

JAVIER. No. I'm not actually.

JONAH. Angela, who's there?

JAVIER. I don't understand, I thought...I thought we were like so...

ANGELA. So did I, I just...

JAVIER. What?

JONAH. Angela? Angela, can you hear me?

(**JONAH** *hangs up phone.*)

ANGELA. My parents are always saying how important experience is. To seeing the world. But everytime I wanna go with them, they say I won't appreciate it till I'm older. So this morning, I thought, Javier, that you were gonna like help me experience so many things. And here we are and the day is almost over and... whatever I was supposed to get from you, Javier—

(**JAVIER** *holds his chest.*)

What is it, what's a matter?

JAVIER. I got this like weight in my chest. Like it's full or filling up.

ANGELA. Where?

JAVIER. All along here.

(**JAVIER** *runs his hand from belly to throat.*)

ANGELA. Do you wanna throw up?

JAVIER. Do you have anything to drink?

ANGELA. There's Sunny D.

JAVIER. No, like to *drink*.

ANGELA. ...

JAVIER. Don't your parents have anything?

ANGELA. ...I think maybe...

> (ANGELA *pulls a half full bottle of shit wine.*)

They use this for cooking sometimes.

> (JAVIER *takes the bottle.*)

I didn't know you drank.

> (JAVIER *uncorks and puts the bottle to his lips, taking it back.*)

I can get you a glass.

JAVIER. I just...I'm just tryin' ta drown him...

ANGELA. ...is it working?

JAVIER. Es like I feel it snaking up my chest, stickin' its acid, wet tongue in from the back uh my throat...

> (JAVIER *coughs up;* ANGELA *offers a napkin.*)

See feel right here, put your hand. You can feel it in my chest slivering through me.

ANGELA. I'm okay.

> (JAVIER *stares at her.*)

What? What is it?

JAVIER. it might feel okay if you let me kiss you again.

ANGELA. We already tried that, Javier, an' it didn't go anywhere.

JAVIER. but this morning, was just a few—I just wanna remember how close...

> (JAVIER *moves close to* ANGELA, *tries to touch her hair.*)

ANGELA. It passed, Javier.

JAVIER. I keep replaying your voice when you said it to me your parents were staying on vacation. So welcoming.

ANGELA. Well they changed their mind, they'll be home any minute. I'm actually on the phone with my Dad from the car.

(The kitchen phone begins beeping, as when left off the hook.)

Please, I'm sorry you feel sick, but—

JAVIER. But you invited me here.

ANGELA. Sometimes, Javier, we visit places, but then we go home.

JAVIER. I just wanna feel what I felt before. So close. Like you an' me were on the same—

ANGELA. People drift. That's what they say.

JAVIER. But we fit so good, our shapes they fit right close like—

ANGELA. Well, I don't want to fit anything, Javier. I just do not. And I'm sorry, I can't help it if that's how I feel. This is my house, Javier, not yours.

(The bottle slips out of JAVIER's hand and smashes. Both him and ANGELA jump, startled. They stare at one another like as though they are a different species. Lights drown out on them.)

(Lights surface up on the alleyway. ADRAY and JONAH sit, still cuffed with their heads turned away, crying. JUANA sits defeated on the floor, EFREN stands downing a Gallo wine. Several moments of them all unable to look at one another.)

ADRAY. Juana...

(ADRAY looks to the mouth of the alley.)

...parent to parent...

JUANA. Efren, their daughter needs them.

EFREN. *(to JUANA)* ¿Donde está la llave?

JUANA. No lo tengo.

(JONAH begins looking for the key frantically.)

JONAH. I have it, it's right here.

(JONAH uncuffs himself.)

Adray, gimme your hands.

(He uncuffs ADRAY.)

ADRAY. Jonah, c'mon.

*(As they exit, **ADRAY** tries to put hoop her arm in **JONAH**'s, he does not let her in. They walk off separate. Lights linger over **EFREN** and **JUANA**.)*

JUANA. Dame el teléfono.

*(**EFREN** tosses the phone to **JUANA**, who opens the phone, the light illuminates her face.)*

EFREN. Juanita, I don't want for you to be disappointed.

JUANA. Ain't him I'm disappointed in.

EFREN. We tried, Juanita. We just wanted him to—

JUANA. I know, Efren. We didn't mean for anything. But here we are.

*(**EFREN** takes a swig of Gallo, then spits it out.)*

EFREN. Fucking snake.

JUANA. I just hope he answers...

*(**JUANA** begins to dial. **EFREN** leans down and they both listen to the receiver with nerves all over. They wait. In the far, distant background, a small voice can be heard to answer. The safety lights flicker out on **JUANA** and **EFREN** both unsure what to say. Curtain.)*

End of Play.